His toughest task yet

"Little angel, you're not being very understanding. And I need you to be the most understanding you can be now."

The Little Angel of Understanding's eyes slowly widened. He smiled just as wide. "You have a task for me, don't you?"

"A hard one."

"Good. I've almost earned all my feathers. This task will finish it off and I'll finally hear the bell that announces my wings."

"Well, don't congratulate yourself too fast." The Archangel of Understanding walked ahead. "Maggie is just about to discover her problem. It won't be easy to fix."

The little angel caught up quickly. "I'm ready to work my best."

Aladdin

Angelwings
№ 7

April Flowers

Donna Jo Napoli
illustrations by Lauren Klementz-Harte

Aladdin Paperbacks
New York London Toronto Sydney Singapore

Thank you to all my family,
Brenda Bowen, Nöelle Paffett-Lugassy, and Richard Tchen

First Aladdin Paperbacks edition March 2000

Aladdin Paperbacks
An imprint of Simon & Schuster
Children's Publishing Division
1230 Avenue of the Americas
New York, NY 10020

ISBN 0-689-83207-9

For Mamma,
with all my love

Angel Talk

"Little angel?" The Archangel of Understanding stood beneath the tree and peered up through the leaves. "I can see your feet. I know you're there."

"Don't look up," the Little Angel of Understanding whispered loudly. "You'll give me away."

"Oh." The archangel squatted and pretended to be examining the base of the tree.

"Is he still near?" whispered the little angel.

The Archangel of Understanding glanced around. "I don't see anyone. Who are you hiding from?"

The little angel climbed down. "The Little Angel of Learning. I don't like him."

"Why not? He seems nice to me."

"Ha. You don't know half the things he

says. He just came back from visiting the Galápagos Islands and he called the plants there 'succulents.'"

The Archangel of Understanding looked puzzled. "What's wrong with that?"

"I've always liked plants."

"So?"

"So he can't call them 'succulents,'" said the little angel. "That's mean."

The archangel laughed. "A succulent is a certain type of plant that holds liquid. Cactuses are succulents."

The little angel smirked. "Why didn't he just say that?"

"Did you tell him you didn't know the word?"

"I didn't have to. No one knows words like that. And I hate it when someone uses a word I don't know."

"Little angel, you're not being very understanding. And I need you to be the most understanding you can be now."

The Little Angel of Understanding's eyes slowly widened. He smiled just as wide. "You have a task for me, don't you?"

"A hard one."

"Good. I've earned almost all my feathers. This task will finish it off, and I'll finally hear the bell that announces my wings."

"Well, don't congratulate yourself too fast." The Archangel of Understanding walked ahead. "Maggie is just about to discover her problem. It won't be easy to fix."

The little angel caught up quickly. "I'm ready to work my best."

Space

Maggie picked up the green porcelain turtle and rubbed it with the soft cloth. When it was perfectly free of dust, she set it down and did the same to the blue glass turtle. There were twenty-two turtles in her collection, and she was cleaning all of them this morning, like she did every Saturday morning.

There, the blue one was finished. And that was the last one.

Maggie went to the window and opened it wide. Autumn weather was just starting. Last night had been the first night that she'd had to close her window in months. Since May, in fact. And, oh, the sugar maple in the DeLucas' side yard had turned overnight. The leaves were bright red now.

The sun glistened off the morning dew on

the grass. It was going to be a perfect day. Maggie would call her friend Shelagh, and they could go exploring down by the creek. It would be fun to try to find frogs and turtles—real turtles—before they went into hibernation.

"Hi." Matthew stood in the doorway on one foot. The other foot was poised in the air, ready to step down into her room. Maggie had worked hard at training Matthew to ask permission before he came bounding in, so it was gratifying to see him standing there like that now. "Can I?"

"Okay. What do you want?"

Matthew jumped into the room. "A water ice."

Maggie laughed. "A water ice? On a cool morning?"

"This is the last Saturday they're serving them till next spring. Mom said I can go to the Co-Op and get one if you or Marcus will walk with me, and Marcus has already said no."

Maggie considered Matthew's fat little

face, which was already smeared with dirt. He'd probably been awake for hours, running around outside like a maniac, and here she was, still in her nightgown. Poor Matthew had way too much energy for his own good. "All right."

"Yay!"

"After I get dressed and have breakfast."

"You're the nicest sister in the world." Matthew kissed Maggie and ran out of the room. "I'll make you breakfast. Just wait," he called over his shoulder.

What awful thing would Matthew make Maggie for breakfast? But she didn't have to eat it if she didn't want to. She did a cartwheel on her rug. Then she got her new sneakers out of the closet.

"Maggie?" Mom came into the room and sat on Maggie's bed. Mom never had liked Maggie's rules about knocking. In fact, Mom never seemed to obey anybody else's rules. "I need your help today."

Maggie groaned. "Do I have to help? I already agreed to take Matthew for a water ice, and then I want to play with Shelagh."

"You can take Matthew first. And there'll be time for Shelagh later. This is important. I have news." Mom's face was serious.

"What is it?" asked Maggie.

"Come here."

Maggie walked over to the bed.

"Sit down beside me, won't you?"

Maggie sat down.

"You know Granny's coming to live with us, right?"

That's all Mom and Dad had talked about for weeks. "Of course. She's coming on the plane tomorrow."

"Right. So we have to get the house set up for her today." Mom made a little smack with her lips. "And last night Dad and I decided that the best solution is for her to be your roommate."

"My roommate? What's that mean?" But

the words slowly made sense to Maggie. "She's going to share my room?" Her voice rose. "She's going to move in here? With me?"

"Right. So we need to bring in the extra bed and bureau and rearrange the furniture in here."

"With me?" said Maggie, shaking her head. "But what about the guest room? It's just right for her."

"That's what we'd been thinking. But Marcus will be twelve next week, and he can't share a room with Matthew forever. It's time he had his own room. So Matthew's moving into the guest room, because it's the smallest and he's little, and Marcus will stay in the boys' room alone."

"But then I'll be the only one who has to share a room."

"You're the only girl and you've had a room all to yourself for years. It's time for you to share."

"But I love my room. I love having things

where they belong. Granny's got too much stuff. Whenever she comes, she sprawls all over the guest room and half the living room, too."

"She's not bringing a lot. And your room has enough space for two."

"It's my space! And the boys' bedroom has even more space."

"Maggie," said Mom with a rising tone. "You love Granny."

"I know." Maggie did love Granny. But that didn't mean she had to give up her privacy. She had the urge to kick something.

"Anyway, Granny has to be in a downstairs room, and only the guest room and your bedroom are downstairs, so that's that."

"I have a better idea," said Maggie. "Granny and Matthew can share this room, and I'll take the guest room. Matthew's the youngest, after all. He should have to share."

"Matthew's a boy."

"So what? He's so little, he doesn't care

about the difference between boys and girls."

Mom's eyes went steely. "But Granny does."

"She's too old to care."

"No, she's not. And that's the end of the conversation, Maggie. I'm not asking you; I'm telling you. Your only choices are how we arrange the furniture."

"There's no space for another bed and another bureau."

"Hmmm. Those shelves over there will have to go." Mom stood up and looked around the room.

"But what about my turtle collection?"

"You can keep it in a box. Or a drawer. . . ." Mom's voice trailed off. "And if we move that mirror to the back of the door, the south wall will be freed up for a bureau. Yes, this will work out fine."

Angel Talk

"Maggie might be nice to her little brother, but boy is she selfish." The Little Angel of Understanding stood in the corner of the bedroom and held out his arms. "Look how big this room is."

"Yes. There's ample room, even with the second bed and bureau they just put in here," said the Archangel of Understanding. "Before, when it had only Maggie's furniture, it was positively capacious."

"What a yucky word: 'capacious.' You sound like the Little Angel of Learning."

"It's a fine word. It means 'roomy.'"

"Then why don't you just say 'roomy'?"

"What's the matter with you today? You've been grumpy since I came to get you."

The little angel felt a flush of embarrassment.

13

It was true: He'd been upset ever since his brief encounter with the Little Angel of Learning this morning. He could still hear the insult the little angel had hurled at him. And the worst part was that he didn't even know what it meant. But that wasn't the archangel's fault; he had no right to take it out on him. "Sorry. Anyway, this girl Maggie needs to learn how to share. Maybe the Little Angel of Generosity could help her more than I can."

"Sharing doesn't seem to be her strong suit, that's for sure," said the archangel. "But I suspect sharing is going to be the smaller of Maggie's problems."

"What do you mean?"

"Maggie's ability to understand is about to be challenged like it never has before. That's why I called you in to help." The archangel put his arm around the little angel's shoulders. "This is going to be a whopper."

Changes

"Granny's here!" Matthew came running through the front door. He zipped around Maggie, grinning like crazy.

Dad followed, with Granny holding on to his arm. "It's an easy step," he said softly to Granny.

"I know the step," Granny snapped. "It's the same step it's always been." She planted her right foot in the threshold. Then she heaved herself up from the porch step with a little "humph" sound. "I can make it the rest of the way by myself."

Mom came forward and kissed Granny on the cheek. "Did you have a good flight?"

"Flights are never good." Granny shook a little, as though to rid herself of the memory.

"Right." Mom's face fell.

Granny looked hard at Mom. Then she gave a little smile that didn't seem quite genuine. "But I guess it was about as good as a bad thing can be."

"I'll get your bags and be right back." Dad ran out to the car again.

Maggie squeezed her hands together. It had been only a few months since she'd last seen Granny, but, oh, what a change. Mom had told her Granny had had a stroke. It was a mild one, but a stroke is serious. That's why Granny couldn't live alone anymore. She didn't have the strength to do lots of things she used to do easily. But Maggie hadn't realized her personality had changed, too. Granny used to be full of smiles. Now she seemed like an old meanie. Maggie would be sharing her bedroom with a sourpuss.

Granny looked straight at Maggie. "Your father told me we're roommates."

Maggie didn't know what to say to that.

Granny kept staring at her, and her face wasn't happy at all.

Maybe Granny was just hungry. Whenever Matthew acted terrible, it was because he was hungry. Maggie gave Granny a quick peck on the cheek. "Dinner's almost ready." She smiled hopefully.

"All right." Granny walked past Maggie into the dining room and sat down.

It wasn't exactly the response Maggie had expected. Dinner wasn't actually completely ready yet. Oh, dear.

"Yay!" called Matthew, hopping around the table.

"Where's the food?" said Granny.

Mom jumped to attention. "Right. Dinnertime. Matthew, come help me serve. Maggie, call Marcus. He's at Craig's house. Tell him to get home quick." She disappeared into the kitchen.

* * *

Dinner was quiet. Mom and Dad asked

Granny a lot of questions at first, but it became clear pretty fast that Granny wasn't in a chatty mood. So everyone concentrated on the chicken and peas and salad.

There was watermelon for dessert.

"I love watermelon," said Matthew.

"Too many seeds," said Granny.

Marcus looked at Maggie. Maggie looked back wordlessly. Matthew made designs with the seeds on his plate, totally happy.

After dinner Dad washed the dishes while everyone else cleared. Granny picked up the salad bowl to carry it into the kitchen.

"Isn't that too heavy for you?" asked Mom.

Marcus took the bowl from Granny.

Granny looked confused for a moment. Then she let her shoulders slump. "I guess you're right. I'll go to bed."

"It's kind of early," said Marcus. "Want to watch TV?"

"You have homework to do, Marcus," said Mom. "No TV for you on a Sunday night."

"I love TV," shouted Matthew. "I'll watch with you, Granny."

"I'm tired," said Granny. She went straight to Maggie's room.

Maggie watched her go, and blinked back tears.

Angel Talk

The little angel gulped. "You didn't prepare me for this. Granny's acting terribly."

"You're right," said the Archangel of Understanding. "She's even more grumpy than you were yesterday."

"That's not fair." The little angel sniffed. "I had a reason. A big one."

"And you think Granny doesn't have a reason for being grumpy?"

"Well, sure. I can imagine how Granny feels—anyone can imagine it. Maggie's bedroom is painted cotton candy pink. And the curtains have mermaids on them. It's a girl's room, not a grandmother's room. So of course it isn't easy for Granny to share that room. But Maggie has to share the room, too. And

Maggie's already acting good about it. Granny's acting so bad, the whole family is in the dumps. Except Matthew."

"Yes. Matthew's imperturbable."

The little angel frowned at the archangel. "Stop that."

The archangel raised his eyebrows innocently. "Stop what?"

"You know what. You're using fancy words just because I hate them."

"It was the right word, little angel. 'Imperturbable' means 'unable to be disturbed.' Matthew seems happy no matter what other people do."

"You're not going to get me to like the Little Angel of Learning just by using a lot of big words like he does."

The Archangel of Understanding smiled. "See how well you understand me?"

"I understand everyone." The little angel threw back his shoulders. "At least when they use ordinary words."

"Really?" The archangel gave the little angel a piercing look. "Everyone? Do you understand Granny? Do you truly believe it's the color of the bedroom and the pattern on the curtains that bother her?"

The Little Angel of Understanding remembered the "humph" noise Granny had made when she'd climbed the step into Maggie's house. And she remembered the sad little groan Granny had made in the middle of dinner. "Now that I think about it, I bet she's upset about more than just sharing a bedroom."

"I think you're right."

"Well, I'm going to find out what," said the little angel.

"Fine. Just don't forget about Maggie in the process. She's the one you're here to help."

Cats

It was already 8:00. Maggie had finished her homework ten minutes ago, but she was waiting to take her bath, because that meant going into the bedroom and facing Granny.

Maggie went into the kitchen and ate another molasses cookie. Mom had made molasses cookies from Granny's old recipe. They were Dad's favorite. Granny hadn't eaten any, though. Not a single one.

It was 8:05. Maybe Maggie would be lucky and Granny would already be asleep. Anyway, Maggie couldn't just eat cookies all night.

She put her homework away in her backpack and walked quietly to her room.

The door was shut.

She stopped outside. Should she knock?

She'd never knocked on her own door before, but now it wasn't her own door, was it?

Maggie cleared her throat.

There was no answer from inside.

Maggie cleared her throat louder.

Still no answer.

Oh, well. Maggie knocked.

"Who is it?" called Granny.

"Me. Maggie."

"Well, come on in. It's your room."

Maggie braced herself for the sight of Granny's clothes and makeup and perfume strewn all over every surface. She opened the door gingerly. But the room was as neat as Maggie always kept it.

Granny sat on her bed with her legs over the side. The small lamp on the bed table cast a dim light. Her big suitcase lay open on the bed beside her. "I wasn't sure which bed was mine. Is this okay?"

"Yes." Maggie went to her own bed and took her nightgown out from under her pillow. "I'm going to take a bath now. Do you need anything?"

Granny straightened the folded edge of the sheet on her bed. "I'll bathe in the morning."

"I have school in the morning. But I'll try my best not to wake you up."

"That's okay," said Granny. "I'm used to getting up early. I have to feed my cats." Her voice caught. "I don't have cats anymore."

Maggie tried to remember Granny's house. It was hard, because Granny always visited them; they hardly ever visited her. But Maggie conjured up the vague image of a big orange cat. "Did you have a lot of cats?"

"Three. Winkin', Blinkin', and Nod."

Maggie laughed. "What nice names. Where are they now?"

"I gave them to Peg. My neighbor." Granny's voice sounded as though she might cry. "I gave away my cats."

"Why? You could have brought them here."

"They're outdoor cats. They'd suffer in the winter up north. I miss them already."

Maggie took a step toward her. "I'm sure they'll be all right."

Granny turned her head away.

Maggie wanted to help, but she didn't know what to do.

"I'll be your cat," said Matthew. He stood in the doorway and looked pleadingly at Maggie.

Maggie nodded.

Matthew got on all fours and crept into the room. He rubbed up against Granny's legs. "Mmmmrrr," said Matthew. Maggie thought it was the worst excuse for a meow that she'd ever heard.

"You're big for a cat," said Granny, but her hand came down lightly on Matthew's head.

Matthew sat on his haunches. "I'm not a normal cat. Couldn't you tell from my growl? I'm a lynx."

"A lynx?" Granny drew her hand back.

"Now how do you even know about lynxes?"

"Mom read me and Maggie a book about a boy who stays on a farm all summer with his cousin or someone. They have a big old mean cat that's really a lynx."

"I think I'd be afraid of a lynx." Granny pulled her legs away now.

"I'm a good lynx," said Matthew. "You don't have to be afraid. As long as you don't try to eat my mice."

Granny opened her mouth, as if to protest.

But Maggie spoke quickly: "It's better he's a lynx than a regular cat."

"Why?"

"Well, if he was a cat, he'd just remind you of Winkin', Blinkin', and Nod, and you'd miss them more. But as a lynx, you can love him." Maggie smiled encouragingly at Granny.

Granny put one finger to her lips. "Love a lynx? Hmmm."

Angel Talk

"Pretty good start, if I do say so myself." The Little Angel of Understanding had to hold back the urge to strut.

"So you made all that happen?"

"It was easy, actually. Matthew's such a willing guy. He was kicking around a ball in his bedroom, and I made that book he talked about fall off the shelf and knock him in the head."

"You made a book knock him in the head? Are you nuts? He could have been hurt."

"It didn't hurt," the little angel said quickly. "It's a paperback book. And then I tossed the book out in the hall and down the stairs."

"What?" The archangel threw his hands out to both sides. "You made a book go flying down the stairs? You can't do things like that. You'll have the whole family fearing the house is haunted."

"Matthew didn't act surprised. He seemed to think nothing of it. He simply followed the book and wound up outside Maggie's room, where he heard Granny say she missed her cats. And the rest just happened naturally."

"You surprise me, little angel." The Archangel of Understanding's voice was a mix of scolding and admiration. "I don't like you making books move all over the place like that. But I have to admit you did a beautiful job with Maggie."

"Maggie? What do you mean?"

"The way she spoke. It was wonderful. How did you get Maggie to realize it was better that Matthew pretend he was a lynx than a regular cat?"

"I didn't. She knew that on her own." The little angel thought about Maggie's words for the first time now. "It was a pretty terrific thing to say, wasn't it? It looks like Maggie's an understanding person all on her own."

"She looked stumped before Matthew appeared, though. I think your timing helped her a lot. Keep it up."

Cold

Maggie went home with Shelagh after school. That helped to make up for the fact that they hadn't been able to play at all on the weekend, because Maggie had been so busy helping set up the bedroom for Granny's arrival. But at 5:00, Maggie headed home. She didn't want to; she did it because that was Mom's rule. Everyone had to help make dinner. Even Matthew would be in the kitchen washing vegetables, or cutting scallions with a pair of scissors or something.

Maggie walked slowly. Would Granny be helping in the kitchen, too?

The late bus that took kids home from athletics stopped at the corner. Marcus got off. He waved to Maggie. That surprised her. Usually Marcus ignored her whenever his friends were around—and the bus was full of his friends. So she felt special and happy at his wave. She ran to catch up with him.

"How's it going?" said Marcus.

"Good. I was just at Shelagh's."

"I thought so. But I mean, how's it going being in the same room with Granny?"

Maggie lifted one shoulder. "I don't know."

"It wasn't my idea, changing rooms and all."

"I know that. Mom told me."

"Bad break," said Marcus.

Maggie thought of how sad Granny's voice had been last night, when she'd talked about her cats. Maggie felt suddenly guilty; she shouldn't be disloyal to Granny. "It'll be okay."

They walked up to the front door side by side. Matthew greeted them with a lynx growl and loped into the kitchen. Maggie followed.

"There you are, sweetie." Mom gave Maggie a kiss on the cheek. "How about you cut the zucchini into rings for me, okay?

Matthew already washed it."

Maggie took out the cutting board and got to work, while Marcus ripped up lettuce for the salad and Matthew sat on the floor leaning against Granny's legs like a sick lynx.

Granny was leaning with both arms on the counter, looking out the window. "Geese," she said.

Mom glanced over from the pot she was stirring on the stove. "Right. They're migrating already."

Matthew climbed up onto the counter and pointed his finger. "Lots of them," he said. "Canada geese."

Maggie put down her knife and came over to watch. The V formation never failed to amaze her. Geese were such funny, orderly creatures. Maggie opened the window so that they could hear the distant honks.

That night Granny unpinned her hair. Two long white braids fell down her back. She pulled one forward over her shoulder and unbraided it.

Maggie couldn't remember ever having seen Granny with her hair down before. "Can I help you?" But she didn't wait for an answer. She settled on Granny's bed behind her and loosened the other braid. "Weren't the geese beautiful today?"

"Horrible is more like it," said Granny.

Maggie scooched on her knees around to the front of Granny. "Why would you say that?"

"Geese leaving means winter's coming."

"I love winter," said Maggie.

"Well, I don't. In the south we don't have harsh winters. Why, I've walked on the beach in January, feeling perfectly comfortable. No, I don't look forward to freezing. My bones clack at the very thought."

"You won't freeze." Maggie shook her head. "We keep the house warm."

But Granny shook her head, too. "Winter is the end of everything."

Angel Talk

Blankets," said the Little Angel of Understanding. "I've got to get Maggie's mom to go out and buy a bunch of extra-warm blankets for Granny."

The Archangel of Understanding didn't say a thing.

"And somehow I've got to find a way to make the dad turn up the thermostat a degree or two." The little angel paced back and forth in front of the archangel. "And maybe Maggie can buy Granny a sweater as a nice autumn surprise."

The archangel put his hand over his mouth.

The little angel paced faster. "And boots, she'll need good boots. And a hat and mittens and—"

The Archangel of Understanding burst out laughing.

"What are you laughing at?"

"You, little angel. You've made yourself a long shopping list."

"So? Someone has to keep Granny warm." The little angel hugged himself. "She said she's afraid of the cold."

"I'm sure she is. And I know for a fact that Maggie's mom has already done a lot of shopping. Don't worry about Granny freezing; she won't."

"Well," said the little angel doubtfully, "I want to do something to help."

"Then pay attention to what's really bothering Granny."

The Little Angel of Understanding thought hard. "Missing her cats and being afraid of the cold are the only complaints she's made—other than saying she hates airplanes and watermelon seeds."

"Those might be the only complaints, but they aren't the only things on her mind."

"Her voice trembles sometimes," said the

little angel slowly. "Especially when she talks about her old home. She must miss everything she left behind so much."

The archangel bowed his head. "The house she raised her children in. The neighbors she's grown old with. Her cats. Even her window boxes full of geraniums."

"Missing what you love can hurt fiercely."

"Yes."

"That's why I'm glad Matthew is pretending to be her lynx." The little angel looked into the archangel's face. "Granny can learn to be happy again if she can replace what she lost."

"I don't know if it's ever possible to replace things, really. But even if you could do that, it wouldn't be enough. There's more to Granny's unhappiness than just missing what she left behind." The Archangel of Understanding tapped the little angel's ears. "Try to remember her words."

And now the little angel replayed Maggie

and Granny's conversation in his head. "Oh, she said winter is the end of everything."

"That's right."

"Oh, now I get it." A feeling of terrific sadness pressed on the little angel's cheeks. "Moving in with Maggie's family makes Granny feel cold, like winter. She feels like her life is coming to an end."

The archangel shivered.

The little angel wrapped his arms around the archangel as though he were the big one and the archangel were the little one. "Granny's wrong," he said firmly.

"What do you mean? Granny's old, little angel. She had a stroke."

"But she's wrong to think that everything is ending. For each thing that ends, something else starts. Wonderful things start."

The Archangel of Understanding wrapped his arms around the little angel, too, so they were hugging each other. "What are you going to do about it?"

"I'm not sure yet, but what you said about Granny's window box back at her old house gave me an idea." The little angel smiled. "You know how much I like plants."

Flowers

The week went by without anything else bad happening between Granny and Maggie. That was partly because Maggie avoided talking to Granny unless she had to. But that was partly because Granny seemed to have adopted a new attitude; instead of complaining, she simply didn't talk.

But something else had been happening all week, something very strange.

When Maggie woke on Tuesday morning, she stood by the window, as she always did upon first waking up. And there on the ground just outside her window was a bouquet of daisies. Maggie ran outside and looked around. The daisies had been thrown there by someone, of course, but there was no one anywhere about. So she took them inside and put them in a vase on the dining room table.

"Where'd they come from?" asked Mom.

"Someone just chucked them in the yard," said Maggie. "Right outside my window."

"How odd." Mom fiddled a little with the flowers, rearranging them by size. "They are nice, aren't they?"

On Wednesday morning there was another bouquet: This time, chrysanthemums. And on Thursday, daylilies.

"Now where did daylilies come from this time of year?" Mom pursed her lips. "Someone must have bought these at a flower shop. I wonder why they threw them away."

Friday's flowers were long-stemmed roses.

"That's it," said Mom at dinner that night. "This is no accident. You must have a secret admirer, Maggie."

"Maggie has a secret admirer?" Marcus almost choked on his spinach. "That's a joke."

45

"And why shouldn't she have a secret admirer?" asked Granny.

Everyone looked at her. It was the longest sentence she'd said in days.

When no one answered, Matthew piped up: "What's a secret admirer?"

"Someone who thinks you're great but doesn't tell you to your face," said Dad.

"Maggie, do you like flowers?" asked Granny.

"Yes."

"So do I." Granny went back to cutting her pork chop.

That night before Maggie crawled into bed, she stood in the dark and looked out the window. Maybe if she woke up super early she could hide behind the curtain and see the person who was bringing the flowers.

"What kind do you think there will be tomorrow?"

Maggie turned her head to see Granny

sitting up in bed. She'd thought she was asleep. "I don't know."

"It's supposed to go down to freezing tonight. Anyone who leaves flowers is a fool." Granny punched her pillow a few times, then lay back. "Winter's coming. And there won't be any more flowers."

In the past week dozens of trees in town had turned yellow and orange and red. The juniper berries and holly berries stood out against the deep green of the bushes. Whatever flowers still stood in people's gardens were browning at the edges. If it really did freeze tonight, those flowers would be totally brown by morning.

Winter didn't have a lot of bright colors, that's for sure.

Maggie rested her cheek against the cold pane of the window glass. "There are flowers *after* winter, though," she said.

But all she heard from Granny was the steady, deep breathing of sleep.

Angel Talk

The flowers are a nice touch," said the Archangel of Understanding.

"Thank you. I have fun waiting to see Maggie's face each day as she discovers the new bouquet."

The archangel smiled. "Good. But I don't really see the point. How do the flowers help anyone?"

"Now you're the one not listening closely enough to Granny," said the little angel.

The archangel jerked his head backward. "What?" Then he tilted his head. "What did Granny say?"

"That there won't be any more flowers once winter comes."

"I heard that. That's why Maggie said there would be flowers after winter."

"Yup." The Little Angel of Understanding put his hands in his pockets and stood tall. "And that's my idea. Or, rather, Maggie's idea. But I led her to it. Flowers after winter."

"I'm still not following you," said the archangel.

"Then watch."

Planting

On Saturday morning when Maggie opened her eyes, Granny was already standing by the window.

"Nothing," she said to Maggie. "Not a single flower."

Maggie's heart dropped. She ran to Granny's side. The ground was covered with frosty dew, but nothing else. The leaves on the lilac bush had withered to brown overnight. The sky was overcast.

"It'll snow soon," said Granny.

"I think you're right. But how can you tell? I thought you lived in the south all your life."

"Not all my life. When I was a girl, I lived in New Jersey. My father ran a paint store in Asbury Park, right down by the ocean."

"Did you hate winter then, too?"

"No." Granny turned and went down the hall to the bathroom.

Maggie watched her go. Then she looked out the window again. The frost on the grass looked different. It seemed as though someone had cleared it away in spots. From Maggie's angle, the cleared parts looked just like a bunch of tulips. Spring flowers.

Maggie ran down the hall. She stood outside the bathroom door. "Did you have a garden, Granny? Did you have flowers in the spring when you lived in New Jersey?"

"Yes."

"Did you have tulips?"

"Yes." After a minute, Granny added, "And daffodils. And hyacinths. And what do you call those funny little flowers in yellow and purple?"

"Crocuses?"

"Yes."

"Well, you're going to have them again." Maggie ran into the kitchen, grabbed Dad by the elbow, and swung him around.

"Careful, Maggie. You'll make me burn these pancakes." Dad eased his elbow away and turned back to the stove. "What's up?"

"I need a lot of money."

"Money?" said Dad.

"Money?" said Marcus, his mouth full of pancake. "I need money, too."

"Did your secret admirer ask to be paid?" said Matthew.

Marcus laughed.

So did Daddy.

"What's so funny?" Mom came into the kitchen holding a catalog with pictures of flowers all over the cover.

Maggie snatched the catalog. "Where did you find this?"

"On the front steps. It's missing an address."

"Well, it's ours," said Maggie, feeling quite sure. "But I don't want to wait for a mail order. I want to go to the hardware store right now and buy bulbs and seeds."

Mom nodded. "That sounds okay. We could use a few new flowers along the border of the house."

"Not just there. Marcus and Matthew and I are going to dig up all the grass in the front yard."

"What?" said Marcus. "Who says?"

"And we're going to plant bulbs. Four hundred of them."

"Four hundred," said Mom weakly. She sat down.

"One hundred each of tulips and daffodils and hyacinths and crocuses."

"I can dig up grass," said Matthew. "Lynxes dig good."

"You're both demented." Marcus reached for another pancake.

"It's for Granny," said Maggie. "She's afraid of winter. But if spring is beautiful, she can be happy about that, at least."

"That's still a lot of work," said Marcus. "Four hundred bulbs? You've got to be kidding."

"If the whole front yard is a garden," said Dad, "then you won't have to mow it, Marcus."

Marcus looked up. "Hey, yeah."

"And we can make paths through it," said Mom. "I love those round patio stones. We can make paths that go in a loop off both sides of the front walk. Anyone who wants to can walk along slowly enjoying flowers on both sides."

Angel Talk

Maggie understands," said the Little Angel of Understanding. "Spring is exactly what Granny needs to look forward to." He extended his hand. "Want to shake my hand? I did it. Those bouquets of flowers got the message across."

The archangel gently pushed the little angel's hand down. "You're not finished yet."

"Why not?"

"You said it yourself. Granny needs to look forward to spring. She has to care about the garden."

"You're right," said the little angel. "Otherwise the garden is just a nice idea, but it doesn't really help her. Maggie has to come to understand that." The Little Angel of Understanding pulled a rose petal out of his pocket and rubbed its velvety thickness between his fingers. "And once Maggie understands, she's got to find a way to get Granny involved."

"You're perspicacious, little angel."

The Little Angel of Understanding looked at the archangel, shocked. "You just called me the same name the Little Angel of Learning called me."

"It's not a bad name," said the archangel. "It means that you have a lot of insight. You understand things well."

"So the Little Angel of Learning wasn't insulting me? Ha." The little angel felt foolish. "How silly of me." He threw the rose petal in the air and blew it. It landed on the archangel's shoulder. "I'm afraid I have a lot to learn before I'll really earn being called that."

"I think you've earned it."

"Thanks," said the little angel. "And now it's time to get back to work and try to earn my wings."

Turtles and Shells

"All those bags?" Granny stood on the front walk and looked at the sacks of bulbs. "You're going to plant all of those?"

"First we have to dig up the grass," said Matthew. "Lynxes have sharp digging claws." He ran to the center of the yard and ripped up grass wildly with his bare hands.

"I'll get the spade," said Marcus. He dug up the grass at the edge of the front walk, then methodically worked across the lawn, inch by inch.

Maggie went to the sidewalk edge and took up where she'd left off before. She had cleared a yard-square patch before they'd even gone to the hardware store to buy the bulbs, because Dad had wanted to pay bills before shopping.

Dad and Mom were now off in the car, going to a nursery to buy patio stones.

It was up to the kids to get rid of the grass. And it was up to Granny to survey their job. Instead, Granny just kept muttering about the number of bulbs. "How many are there in these bags, anyway?" she asked.

"Four hundred," said Matthew.

"Six hundred, actually," called Maggie. "Besides tulips and daffodils and hyacinths and crocuses, we bought some lilies and liatris and iris and allium. And, oh, yes, Oriental poppies. And then things I can't remember. We got some of everything."

Matthew came over to Maggie. "Can I see your trowel?"

Maggie held up her trowel.

Matthew grabbed it and ran back to his digging spot. "Sometimes lynxes use tools," he shouted back at her.

Maggie put her hands on her hips and was about to argue with Matthew. Then she saw how much faster Marcus was working with the spade than she'd been working with the trowel. She headed for the garage.

Granny followed. "What're you doing?"

"There's a shovel in here somewhere." Maggie turned on the light. "Here it is."

"Are you strong enough to use it?" Granny's voice had an edge of wistfulness.

"Sure." Maggie pulled the shovel off the hook and swung it to the ground.

Clank.

"Oh, look. I knocked down another trowel. I didn't even know we had two trowels. Would you like to use it, Granny?"

"Me? If I got down on these old knees, I might never get up again."

Maggie hurried back to her spot and worked as hard and as fast as she could.

A couple of hours later, Mom and Dad came home. They unloaded stacks of round patio stones onto the front walk. Then they unloaded fifty-pound bags of bark chips.

"What're the chips for?" asked Marcus suspiciously.

"After we plant the bulbs, we'll need to cover the bare dirt with chips so it doesn't just all turn to dust and hard clay," said Dad. "Don't worry. Your job is over as soon as the grass is gone. That's plenty of work for you kids."

"I want to help do all the jobs," said Maggie. "The garden was my idea, after all."

"All right," said Dad. "I won't turn down help."

Granny went inside. She came out a few minutes later and whispered to Mom, who was digging up grass with the extra trowel. Mom went back into the house with her. They both came out again, with Mom carrying a tray stacked with glasses and a pitcher. "Granny made lemonade," said Mom. She laughed. "We're all sweating as though it's summer. So lemonade is just right."

The lemonade was sweet and delicious.

Maggie finished her glass and went back to work.

It was dinnertime before the last patch of grass finally disappeared.

"I'm done," said Marcus. He fell in the dirt in a dramatic swoon. "Don't ever ask me to help with anything again."

"Come over here and jump on this, Matthew," said Dad. He had just put the last patio stone in place. "Test it to see if it wobbles."

Matthew hopped on the stone.

"Perfect," said Dad. "That's enough for one day."

"Everyone to the showers," said Mom. "Or you won't be allowed at the dinner table."

Maggie took Granny's hand. "Will you help me put the tools away?"

Granny gave a brief nod. "Of course." She picked up the trowels. "Was this garden really your idea?"

"Yes. Spring will be glorious, Granny. And you know what?"

"What?"

"You can't have a glorious spring without winter first."

Maggie woke to high-pitched clinking noises. She rolled over and looked at Granny.

Granny smiled at her and held her hand up, dangling a crossed set of sticks with strings hanging down. Each string had seashells attached to it. Granny waved the contraption over Maggie. It sang in that clinking, tinkling way. "It's a wind chime," said Granny.

"Where did it come from?"

"I made it last night after you fell asleep."

Maggie sat up and examined the wind chime. "Where did you get all these shells?"

"I have a collection. I've saved shells all my adult life. I don't have anywhere to display them here, so I keep them in one of my suitcases. Want to see?"

"Sure. And I'll show you my turtle collection. It's in a box in the closet."

"I'd like to see it," said Granny. She set the wind chime down on Maggie's bed.

"What are you going to do with the wind chime?"

"I thought it could hang from a tree in the front yard. Every garden needs music, don't you think?"

Maggie smiled wide. "It's perfect. And you know, it's stupid for my turtles to be hidden in the closet. They'd love to hide in the garden instead."

"You're full of good ideas," said Granny.

Angel Thoughts

The newest Archangel of Understanding sat in the tree in the front yard and watched Granny direct Maggie about where to plant the various bulbs. It turned out that Granny remembered an awful lot more about spring gardens than she had expected.

The wind chime rang out below the archangel like a heavenly bell. It was with the first ringing of that chime that the angel's wings had fully feathered out.

He gave one last look at Granny and Maggie and flew off. There was a certain Little Angel of Learning that he wanted to talk with. And if that little angel used any words he didn't know, he was determined to swallow his pride and ask what they meant. After all, the little

angel probably used those words because they were the right words—not because he wanted to show off. Maybe if the archangel hung around him a bit, his own vocabulary would grow. But even if it didn't, he'd have a new friend, and that was what it was all about.

How to plant a tulip

Tulips are the most popular spring flowers. Instead of starting from a seed like other plants, tulips start from a bulb. The bulb is planted in the ground (or in a pot). It's easy to grow beautiful tulips for spring. If you'd like to try, here are some things you'll need to know:

Location
Tulips grow best in a sunny location. To prevent the plants from falling over during heavy winds, plant bulbs in areas that are protected.

Soil
All you need is reasonably good, moist soil if you are planting outdoors. For indoor planting, use a commercial potting soil.

Planting

If you are planting tulips outside, you'll have to plant them in the fall season (for spring flowers). But if you want to plant tulips in an indoor pot, you can have tulips any time of year.

For most larger bulbs, make a hole in the soil five to six inches deep. Smaller bulbs can be planted four inches deep. Put the bulb into the hole, and cover loosely with soil.

Outdoor tulips will be watered by the rain; indoor tulips you'll have to remember to water, at least once a week.

Time flies—winter today, spring tomorrow. Plant a few tulip bulbs around your house this fall, and next spring you'll be glad you did.

Read all of the
Aladdin *Angelwings* stories:

№. 1

Friends Everywhere
0-689-82694-X

№. 2

Little Creatures
0-689-82695-8

№. 3

On Her Own
0-689-82985-X

№.4

One Leap Forward
0-689-82986-8

№.5

Give and Take
0-689-83205-2

№.6

No Fair!
0-689-83206-0

All titles $3.99 US / $5.50 Canadian

Aladdin Paperbacks
Simon & Schuster Children's Publishing
www.SimonSaysKids.com

And don't miss these other
Aladdin *Angelwings* stories:

№·8
Playing Games

№·9
Lies and Lemons

№·10
Running Away